PRESENTED BY

Brooke Ransom

Grumley the Grouch

by Marjorie Weinman Sharmat
illustrated by Kay Chorao

Holiday House · New York

Library of Congress Cataloging in Publication Data

Sharmat, Marjorie Weinman.
  Grumley the grouch.
  SUMMARY: J. Grumley Badger, biggest grouch in
the neighborhood, becomes more and more pleasant
when he meets Brunhilda Badger.
  [1. Friendship—Fiction. 2. Badgers—Fiction.
3. Animals—Fiction] I. Chorao, Kay. II. Title.
PZ7.S5299Gs   [E]   79-28290
ISBN 0-8234-0410-2

*For Roz and Brandon,
the stars of Garth Road*

J. Grumley Badger was the biggest grouch in the neighborhood.

Every day he found at least ten things he didn't like.

"How are you, Grumley?" his neighbor Hank Musk-rat would ask politely.

"Simply terrible," Grumley would reply.

"How are things going, Grumley?" asked another neighbor, Nero Pig.

"Rotten," said Grumley.

"The sun is too shiny.

The rain is too wet.

The grass isn't green enough.

The sky is too far up."

Grumley gnashed his teeth. "And there's more," he said. "Much more."

One rainy day Grumley's house got flooded.

"I knew the rain was too wet," he muttered as he sloshed through his house.

"Slosh! Slop! And a soggy bed! Things never get better. They only get wetter."

Grumley went to Hank's house.

"I'll have to stay with you until my house dries out," he said. And he moved in.

"I always liked your place," said Grumley.

"You did?" asked Hank.

"Of course it could be better," said Grumley.

"Oh?" said Hank. "How?"

"Well, your floor squeaks," said Grumley.

"I never noticed," said Hank.

"And your mattress sags," said Grumley.

"I never noticed that either," said Hank.

"Yes, it just sags and sags," said Grumley. "Do you mind if I sleep on your floor? I prefer a squeak to a sag."

Grumley lay down on the floor. He looked up at the ceiling. "I suppose you know about your ceiling," he said.

"What about it?" asked Hank.

"It has water spots," said Grumley. "And they're very ugly."

"Take a nap, Grumley," said Hank.

"Do you expect me to nap under ugly water spots?" said Grumley. "Don't you remember what happened to my house?"

"How can I forget?" said Hank. "Your house flooded,
and you came to stay with me."

"Aren't you happy to have me, Hank?" asked Grumley.

"Um," said Hank.

"*Um*?" cried Grumley. "Um means you're not happy
to have me."

Grumley got up. "I'm leaving!" he said, and he walked out and slammed the door.

He went to Nero Pig's house.

"Say Nero, did you hear about my wet house?" asked Grumley.

"Yes, and it made me so sad I couldn't eat for two hours," said Nero. "Would you like to stay with me until your house is dry?"

"I accept," said Grumley.

Grumley went inside and walked around. "I have never been inside your house," he said. "Your floors don't squeak, your ceiling looks spotless, and your mattress is firm."

"Glad you like everything," said Nero.

"I didn't say *that*," said Grumley. "Your clock ticks ferociously, there is a horrid draft from your kitchen window, and the unmistakable smell of rotting artichokes is in the air."

Nero opened a book and started to read.

"Why don't you say something?" said Grumley.

Nero kept reading.

"If you don't talk to me, I'll leave," said Grumley.

Nero read on.

"I'm leaving!" said Grumley, and he walked out and slammed the door.

He stood outside the door. He didn't know where to go next.

He started to walk. "Maybe I'll just walk around until my house dries," he thought.

Grumley walked for many miles. He was feeling very tired when he saw a house by the side of the road. He went up the front walk. There was a sign on the door. GO AWAY.

Grumley gnashed his teeth. "I do not like that sign," he said. "I do not like the way it looks. I do not like what it says. I do not like anything about it. But I am so tired that I will knock on the door anyway."

Grumley knocked.

Brunhilda Badger answered the door. She pointed to the sign. "I don't like strangers," she said.

GO
AWAY

signed:
Brunhilda

"I am tired," said Grumley.

"I don't like tired strangers either," said Brunhilda.

"Well then, I'm cold and hungry," said Grumley.

"I don't like tired or cold or hungry strangers," said Brunhilda. "And I also don't like them when they're rested, warm, and fed."

"May I come in anyway?" asked Grumley.

"If you must," said Brunhilda.

Grumley walked inside and stood in front of the fire-place. "Your fire feels nice and toasty," he said.

"It's too hot," said Brunhilda.

"Grumley saw some soup in a pot. "That might warm me up, too," he said.

"It's greasy and gucky," said Brunhilda.

Grumley saw a pillow on the floor. "That pillow would be fine for a weary head," he said.

"It's lumpy," said Brunhilda.

Grumley looked at Brunhilda. "Don't you like anything?" he asked.

"Well, there is so much not to like," said Brunhilda.

"I agree," said Grumley. "But there must be something you like."

"I'll think about it," said Brunhilda.

"Well . . ." said Grumley.

"It's very difficult, you know," said Brunhilda. "But I *am* thinking about it." Then she said, "I remember. Once I liked chocolate sundaes with walnuts and cherries."

"Me, too," said Grumley. "With marshmallow bits on top."

"I think I'll make one," said Brunhilda.

"Two, please," said Grumley.

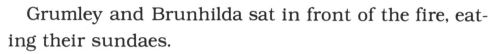

Grumley and Brunhilda sat in front of the fire, eating their sundaes.

Grumley said, "Something very strange is happening."

"I know it," said Brunhilda.

"I like *you*," said Grumley. "That's what's strange."

"I like you, too," said Brunhilda.

"Do you suppose there are even more things to like besides each other and sundaes?" asked Grumley.

"Could be," said Brunhilda. Then she said, "How about soft shirts? I like soft shirts under scratchy ones."

"I like picture frames when I have a picture," said Grumley.

"I like holes," said Brunhilda. "They're airy and cool, and you can see through them."

"I like breathing," said Grumley.

"That's a good one," said Brunhilda. "How about rain? Maybe we could like rain."

"Rain? Rain's too wet," said Grumley.

"But rain comes before a rainbow," said Brunhilda.

"I suppose," said Grumley. "There was a rainbow when I went to stay with Hank Muskrat. He let me stay in his house and on his mattress and on his floor."

"I could like Hank," said Brunhilda.

"Yes, Hank is somebody to like," said Grumley. "And Nero Pig also said I could stay with him. He couldn't eat for two hours when he heard about my soaked house."

"I could like Nero, too," said Brunhilda.

"Yes, so could I," said Grumley.

"Let's tell Hank and Nero," said Brunhilda.

"It's a long walk to their houses," said Grumley.

"I think I like long walks," said Brunhilda.

"I think I do, too," said Grumley.

Grumley and Brunhilda started to walk.

"I'm definitely liking this," said Grumley, as they walked along.

"Yes," said Brunhilda. "The pebbles and the trees are all first-rate."

"The dirt under our feet isn't bad at all," said Grumley.

"And let's not forget the clouds up there," said Brunhilda. "They remind me a bit of soft shirts, and I know I like soft shirts."

"I like the company the best of all," said Grumley.

"Yes. The very best of all," said Brunhilda.

Suddenly Grumley saw Hank and Nero sitting in front of Nero's house. Grumley and Brunhilda ran up to them.

"We were just talking about you, Grumley," said Nero. "We think you're the biggest grouch in the neighborhood."

"No doubt about it," said Hank.

"No, he's not," said Brunhilda. "He likes dirt and sundaes and me, Brunhilda, and picture frames and all kinds of things."

"How about sagging mattresses?" asked Hank.

"And the unmistakable smell of rotting artichokes?" asked Nero.

"Well, maybe," said Grumley. "But not as much as I like all of you."

Hank and Nero put their heads together and whispered.

"That doesn't sound like a grouch talking," said Nero.

"That's positively non-grouch talk," said Hank.

"Let's all go to my house for good conversation and chocolate sundaes," said Grumley. "My house must be dry by now."

Grumley, Brunhilda, Hank, and Nero went to Grumley's house and stepped inside.

The floor was still flooded. Water dripped from the ceiling.

Grumley sloshed around.

"Well, well, well, it's still not quite dry," he said cheerfully.

"Dry isn't everything," said Brunhilda as she wrung out her dress. "Let's all sit on this soggy sofa and enjoy our sundaes."

Two months later, when the house dried out, Brunhilda and Grumley got married.

Grumley became less and less grouchy as the years went by, but still . . .

He never became terribly fond of rain.